The Goosehill Gang
and the
May Basket Mystery

by Mary Blount Christian
illustrated by Betty Wind

Do not judge by appearances, judge with right judgment.
John 7:24 RSV

Publishing House
St. Louis

In memory of my aunt and namesake

Concordia Publishing House, St. Louis, Missouri
Copyright © 1978 Concordia Publishing House
Manufactured in the United States of America

Library of Congress Cataloging in Publication Data

Christian, Mary Blount.
    The Goosehill Gang and the May basket mystery.

    SUMMARY: Pete decides that the family next door are "weirdos" because they
never speak, but learns along with the other members of his gang that the family is not
weird but handicapped.
    [1. Deaf—Fiction. 2. Mutism—Fiction.
3. Physically handicapped—Fiction. 4. Christian life
—Fiction] I. Wind, Betty. II. Title.
PZ7.C4528Gox   [Fic]   78-2443
ISBN 0-570-07359-6

"And hurry!" Pete told Beth over the phone. "Get the rest of the gang. The moving van is already there." Within minutes Beth, along with Tubby, Marcus, and Don, eagerly watched as the van doors opened. The men began carrying boxes and furniture into the vacant house next door.

"Remember what we're watching for," Tubby reminded the other members of the Goosehill Gang. "Bicycles, skate boards—anything that will tell us there will be a new kid in the neighborhood."

"Even cribs or playpens that might mean babysitting jobs," Beth added practically. The boys nodded, not taking their eyes off the movement next door.

"That stuff looks old and really heavy," Don said. "Look how those men are struggling with that chest of drawers."

Beth nodded. "It looks like some of the stuff at the museum."

"Look!" Don said. "There's a crib . . . I think. Isn't it funny looking?"

Pete scratched his chin. "No. That's a cradle. It could be for a tiny baby. Or maybe it's a doll cradle for a girl."

Beth twirled one of her pigtails as she watched. "It looks awfully heavy. I don't think it's for dolls, though. It's sort of like that real baby cradle that I've seen at the museum."

When the men had finished unloading Don sighed. "I don't think they have any children, do you?"

"No," Pete agreed. "I guess not many people with kids in school would be moving this near the end of the school year anyway."

"Look!" Don whispered. "A car just drove up." The children watched as a couple got from the car. Silently, and without looking to the right or left, they walked inside the house. The moving van pulled away. "They looked about the age of my grandmother," Tubby said. "I guess they wouldn't have any kids, after all."

The children stood and stretched and moved onto the porch. "Oh, well," Pete said. "It was kind of fun watching the movers anyway. Saturdays get kind of dull without anything to do."

The children decided to wait and greet the new neighbors after they'd had a chance to settle down and unpack. But the days drifted by and they forgot about it.

"That's the quietest house," Pete said one day. "I bet they don't like children. Of course I'm too old to make much noise. But Norman and Nancy are little and noisy."

Beth nodded. "Have you noticed the yard? They've planted so many flowers since they moved in. And it's so neat! I bet they wouldn't want us tracking across it."

"Yeah," Pete said. "They aren't friendly at all. Lots of times they are working in the yard and I go by and speak. But they don't say anything back."

"Has your mother met them?" Marcus asked.

8

Pete nodded. "Yeah. I asked her what they were like. But she said I should make an effort to find out. She said if I'm so nosey I shouldn't try to use somebody else's nose."

Beth giggled. "Well, they might try to chop yours off!"

Pete laughed. "Yeah. I mean after all they didn't speak, even when I spoke first."

"What are their names? Did your mother tell you?" Don wanted to know. Pete shook his head. "No, but I looked on their mailbox when they were gone. It's Palacik."

The next morning was the first of May. Pete dressed for school and went to get the newspaper for his father while his mother put breakfast on the table.

He blinked and rubbed his eyes. Maybe he was still half asleep, he told himself. But what an odd thing to see! Pete leaned closer. There was a basket of flowers hanging on his front door knob.

The basket was filled with flowers of every description. He lifted it from the knob and carried it inside. "Look, Mom!" he called. "Look what I found hanging on our front door."

"Ummmmm," Mrs. Davis said. "They smell so sweet. Is there a card? What does it say?"

Pete ran his fingers around the edge of the basket. "No. I don't see a card. Who could have sent these?"

Nancy and Norman skipped in to eat their breakfasts. They slid into their chairs. Norman was interested in breakfast, but Nancy was more interested in the basket of flowers. "Grammy's flowers," Nancy said.

"Naw!" Pete said. "Grandmother lives in another state. If she sent us flowers she'd have to ship them. There's no shipping tag on these."

Mrs. Davis laughed. "Oh, Nancy! I believe you're right. But for the life of me I don't know why!"

Pete scratched his head and looked at his mother and sister. "Huh?" he asked.

Mrs. Davis patted her son's shoulder. "I tell you what. Why don't you make this a case for the Goosehill Gang. Surely you can come up with the answer. And it just might surprise you!"

Pete agreed. At school that morning he told the children about the basket. "Did any of you do it?" he asked. But the other children were surprised. None of them had gotten any flowers. "Then Nancy must be right," Pete said. "They must be from my grandmother. But how?"

"Maybe that's the surprise your mom meant. Maybe your grandmother is in town," Don suggested.

"I don't think so," Pete replied. "The twins aren't very good at secrets. If Grandmother was in town, I think they'd tell me."

"Didn't Nancy almost say that? Didn't she say, 'Grammy's flowers?'"

"Not really," Pete corrected. "She said, 'Grammy's flowers,' all right. But she calls our grandmother Gramma, not Grammy!"

Tubby spoke up, "When I was little and didn't see my grandmother much, I'd forget what I called her. Maybe Nancy forgot and changed."

"Maybe," Pete said. "But she talks on the phone to grandmother once a week. And one week's not enough time to forget, even if you're a little kid like Nancy."

Don snapped his fingers. "That's it! The phone! I saw an advertisement on television once. It said you can phone flowers to another city!"

Tubby threw back his head in laughter. "Oh, really, Don. You're not trying to tell us that flowers can travel through those little wires!"

Don laughed. "No. But there's some way you can order them in your town. And the florist in another town will deliver them."

"Pete, let's check with the florist!" Beth suggested. "Maybe he will tell us if someone ordered them."

After school the Goosehill Gang stopped by the florist. The woman listened, then said, "I'll check my order book just to make sure. But I don't remember such an order." She leaned over, studying her book while the children walked around looking at the different plants and cut flowers.

The woman shook her head. "No. I was right. I didn't get any order from out of town. Maybe they are from someone's own garden."

"You mean like homegrown and delivered?" Pete asked.

The woman nodded. "Flowers have a way of speaking to you, you know. You just have to know the language."

"Huh," Tubby wondered. "You mean flowers talk? I never heard them say anything."

Beth laughed. "I think if I did I'd run like a scared goose!"

The woman laughed. "No, they don't speak in words. But many flowers are symbols of words. I

don't remember them all, but for instance, if you wanted to tell someone you share their sad times as well as their glad times, you would send them roses."

Beth sniffed dreamily at one of the plants. "Oh, I like that idea. Sad times, glad times—that's a real friend."

"Where could we find out more?" Marcus asked. "Do you think the library could help?"

The woman pulled an orchid from the cold storage box. She began twisting lace and ribbon around it. "Yes, I think maybe it could."

The children thanked her and started to leave. "Oh, wait!" she called to them. "This orchid just reminded me of something. Just this morning I delivered an orchid and some lilacs to an address. I

was paid early and told just to leave them on the doorstep without ringing. It was almost dawn when I made the delivery."

"Wow!" Beth said. "Isn't that an odd combination of flowers?"

"Yes," the woman agreed. "And something else. I make the same delivery once a year. On May 1 in fact."

"Could you tell us who?" Pete asked. "Maybe then we'd have a clue to our own flowers."

"I'm not sure . . ." the woman hesitated. "Oh, he's a friendly man. I'm sure he wouldn't mind." Hastily she wrote a name and address on the back of one of her advertising cards.

Again the children thanked her and left. "The address is on the way to the library," Tubby said. "Why don't we stop there first?"

In a few minutes the children rang the doorbell. A woman answered. When the children asked for Mr. Anderson she told them he was at work. "I'm Mrs. Anderson. May I help you?"

When Pete explained the woman nodded. "I understand. Come in and I'll show you." She showed them a glass basket with the orchid centering a bunch of lilacs. "The orchid is a more rare flower," she explained. "It tells me that our love is rare. In early Europe young men would go great distances to gather rare flowers in order to prove their love."

Tubby grinned. "Wow, Pete. Do you think somebody is trying to tell you they love you?"

Pete felt his cheeks grow red. He stammered, then asked, "But what about the lilacs? Do they have a message too?"

The woman nodded. "They ask, 'Do you love me?'"

"Oh, how beautiful," Beth said. "But the florist said the delivery is always May 1. Is that your anniversary?"

The woman held up her hands, palms up. "Why, no. It's because it is May 1. It's tradition!

"I . . . I don't understand," Pete said. "Why is May 1 so special?"

"My husband and I both are from families that still strongly live the old European traditions. We keep them alive because they are beautiful. It seems a shame for them to fade and die."

She pulled a scrapbook from a nearby shelf and opened it to several yellowed photographs. "See? This is my grandmother. She danced the May pole dance. There are streamers of flowers in her hair. The young men brought back a tall, straight young

tree and decorated it with flowers and ribbons. The young girls wove a pattern from the streamers by weaving in and out as they skipped around the pole."

Beth's eyes lighted up. "Oh, my mother said they used to dance in a May fete at school. I don't know why they stopped doing it."

The woman sighed. "Yes, sometimes busy people find it hard to keep a tradition going. But the basket of flowers is still a simple and lovely thing to do."

The children thanked her and left. At the library they found a list of flower messages.

"Anemones mean 'go away and leave me alone,'" Tubby read. "Did you have any anemones in the basket?"

Beth pointed to the picture of the gladiola. "Look, it is like a knife. It means someone has pierced your heart."

"They are kind of like valentines, aren't they?" Tubby asked the others. "But what about your basket, Pete?"

"Here it is," Marcus said. "Mixed bunches! They are a cheery greeting to a good friend."

Tubby laughed. "Too bad, Pete. I guess you are just a friend and not a love."

The children replaced the book on the shelf and started toward Pete's house. "We have to go about this the right way," Pete said. "We've been trying to find out what the flowers mean, but maybe we need to find out who they are from to find out what they mean.

"I think we will have to identify the flowers, then look in yards to see who is growing those kinds of flowers," he finished. At Pete's the children tried to identify each kind of bloom in the basket. They wrote them down. Then they split up. Each of them walked along one block. They tried to find the yard that contained all of the flowers in the basket.

In an hour they met at Pete's. "It's no use," Tubby said, puffing hard. "I would find a yard with

roses but no iris. If it had iris it didn't have mock orange. None of the yards had all of the flowers." Don and Beth nodded. They didn't have any luck either.

"Well, I think I have a surprise," Pete said. "The only yard that I found with all of the flowers is next door. It is the Palacik's yard."

The children gasped. "But you said they were so unfriendly! And you said they didn't like children!" Beth reminded him.

Pete shrugged. "I can't help that. It's the only yard that matches. Mom!" Pete called. "I'm going next door a few minutes."

Nancy bounced in. "I want to go, Pete. I want to go to Grammy's."

"Not Grammy's, Nancy. I'm going next door."

"Uh huh, Pete. It's Grammy's," Nancy argued. Pete shrugged and motioned for the others to follow.

They stepped onto the Palacik's porch. Nancy pushed the doorbell before Pete had a chance. "It doesn't work," Pete said. "I didn't hear it ring."

"Uh huh," Nancy said. "It's a door light!"

Pete shrugged and rolled his eyes. "My sister, the nut! A doorlight indeed." But even as he spoke the door opened. The woman nodded to them and

reached down to hug Nancy. She motioned them inside. Nancy ran into the den and climbed on the man's lap. She gave him a big hug.

Tubby laughed. "It looks like your baby sister hasn't had any trouble making friends, Pete."

But Beth didn't speak. She was carefully studying each piece of furniture. "It looks just like the early American room at the museum," she cooed. "It's so . . . beautiful!"

"Grammy and Grampy don't hear, Pete," Nancy said. "They don't talk either. You talk to them like this!" She wiggled her pudgy fingers. "But I don't know how yet."

"Wow!" Pete said. "No wonder they never looked up when I spoke. No wonder the house seemed so quiet."

About that time a light flashed several times. "See, Pete?" Nancy said, "A doorlight!"

Tubby laughed again. "Pete, I think from now on you'd better listen to what Nancy says."

A young girl came in. She hugged Mr. Palacik. "Hi!" she greeted the children. "Hello, Nancy. You must be ready to learn a new word today."

She quickly made a signal with her fingers. "Milk!" she told Nancy.

Nancy mimicked her. "Milk!" Nancy repeated.

"You're Pete, aren't you?" the girl said, quickly making hand motions as she spoke. "I'm Katy Palacik. These are my grandparents." The couple

nodded and shook hands as the children spoke their own names and the girl repeated them in sign language.

"I . . . I feel so awfully stupid," Pete said. "I guess I just made up my mind that they didn't like kids because they were so quiet."

The girl nodded as she repeated for her grandparents. "Yes. I guess all this museum furniture turns off lots of kids, too. They sort of think of them as ancient."

"But it's so beautiful!" Beth protested. "Please! What happened to the cradle? I'd love a closer look!"

When Katy had repeated to her grandparents, the girls went into a small bedroom. It held a canopy bed and a heavy dresser with hurricane lamps. The cradle was in the corner. A glass-faced cloth doll dressed in a long ruffled gown lay in it.

"Oh!" Beth cooed. "May I?" The girl nodded and Beth picked up the doll. She cradled it and swayed slightly left and right.

Katy grinned. "I'm the same way. I think I'm too old for dolls, but I can't resist her. These things have belonged to Palaciks for generations. I guess someday I'll be keeping them for my grandchildren."

The children looked and touched and examined every piece of furniture. They stared at the pictures in the stereopticon that the Palaciks showed them. "I think I could step right into the picture, it's so real!" Don marveled. "This is better than television."

When the children started to leave they each shook hands with the Palaciks. Mrs. Palacik waggled her fingers, then looked toward Katy. "She said you are welcome anytime. She says they love children and want to be friends," Katy interpreted.

Pete grinned. "I know that now. I'm sorry I've been such a goof."

At home he searched the yard until he found some jasmine. He put it on the Palaciks' front steps. Pete remembered that it meant "our friendship is true and will last."

Later Mrs. Davis asked her son, "Does it worry you that you can't talk to the Palaciks?"

"Oh, I plan to learn as much sign language as possible," he told her. "And if that fails, I'm still not worried. There are flowers for every occasion!"

Mrs. Davis gave her son a big hug. And they both reached down to give Nancy an extra special one.